Baron Munchhausen

His Wonderful Travels and Adventures

Retold by ERICH KASTNER

Translated by RICHARD AND CLARA WINSTON

Illustrated by WALTER TRIER

HARLEQUIN BOOKS

JULIAN MESSNER, INC.   NEW YORK

Published by Julian Messner, Inc.
8 West 40 Street, New York 18

Published simultaneously in Canada
by The Copp Clark Publishing Co. Limited

PRINTED IN THE UNITED STATES OF AMERICA
LIBRARY OF CONGRESS CATALOG CARD NO. 57-11502

FOREWORD

One fact is clear, firm and solid as a rock: Baron Münchhausen actually and really lived, just about two hundred years ago. He was born in the part of Germany known as Braunschweig, his first name was Hieronymus, and he became an army officer almost as soon as he finished school. In those days that was the usual career of nobility. Their fathers lived on estates, went hunting and riding, drank red punch, and sent their sons off to be army officers. When the fathers reached old age, they called the sons back home. And then the sons in turn went hunting and riding, drank red punch, and sent their sons off to be army officers.

In America those were the days before the Revolution, and in Europe the days when Empress Maria Theresa reigned in Austria, Frederick the Great in Prussia, and Catherine II in Russia. Since there were wars in all parts of Europe, there were armies everywhere, and since there were armies everywhere, officers were much in demand. If there did not happen to be a war going on in their own country, they would ride to some other country where there was one, and enlist in that country's army.

This is exactly what Hieronymus von Münchhausen did. When he became bored with staying home, he enlisted in the Russian army. In the war between Russia and Turkey he was taken prisoner and held captive for several years. After his release his old father called him back to Badenwerder, which was the name of their estate and little castle, and thereafter Hieronymus was the master. He took off his uniform, went hunting and riding, and drank red punch. As it happened, he had no sons, so he was not able to send them forth to be officers.

So he lived just like the other barons, and today that's all we'd know about him, if he had not told amazing stories over the punch bowl. Such amazing tales that the other barons, the pastor, the doctor and the magistrate, who sat at table with him, gaped and gawked. Such amazing stories that somebody secretly wrote them down and had them printed. Münchhausen was highly annoyed and tried to put a stop to the printing. When he found that he could not, he died of apoplexy.

Now what was there so amazing about those stories? They are full of the wildest imagining! In the middle of stories about places he had really seen on his travels, and about wars in which he had really taken part, Münchhausen would produce fantasies that made the rafters ring. Is it, then, possible to become famous by telling wild tales? Certainly. But only when the tales are as funny, as fantastic, as straight-faced and as cunning as Münchhausen's — told not to fool the listener, but to entertain him.

So don't come home and say: "Just imagine, Mama, I was having a talk with a car, and the car said it thought it is going to rain." You won't win fame with such tales. Storytelling like Münchhausen is an art, and you really had better not try to imitate it. Instead do your homework and when it's all done, read about Münchhausen's "Wonderful Adventures."

The Horse On The Church Tower

I set out on my first trip to Russia in the depths of winter. For in spring and fall the roads in Poland, Courland and Latvia are so muddy that it is impossible to make any progress, and in summer they are so bone-dry and dusty that you choke and cough all the time. Therefore I traveled in winter, and on horseback, since that is the most practical way to go. Unfortunately, I felt colder and colder every day, for I was wearing only a thin coat, and the whole land was so covered with snow that I frequently saw no trace of a road, no signposts, nothing but snow, snow, snow.

One evening, stiff and tired, I dismounted from my good steed, and fastened the halter to a branch of a tree that was sticking up out of the snow. Then I lay down on my coat, my pistol under my arm, and fell asleep.

When I awoke, the sun was shining. And when I looked around, I had to rub my eyes. For there I was right in the middle of a village. Moreover, I had been sleeping in the cemetery. Thunder and Blitzen, I thought, for what healthy — even if half frozen — man likes the idea of sleeping in a churchyard. My horse had disappeared. And yet I had staked him carefully right beside me.

Suddenly I heard a loud whinnying high above my head. I looked up and saw the poor animal dangling from the weathervane of the church tower. It was whinnying and kicking wildly; naturally, it didn't find the position very comfortable. But how in the world had it got up there on the church tower?

Slowly, the explanation dawned on me. Village and church had been completely snowed in, and what I had in the darkness taken for a branch of a tree was in fact the weathervane of the village church. During the night the weather changed. There had been a sudden thaw and I had sunk down, inch by inch, along with the melting snow, until I woke up among the gravestones.

What was I to do now? Since I am a good shot, I took my pistol, aimed at the halter, and shot it in two. The horse fell upon the soft earth of the cemetery quite unharmed, and very happy he was to have solid ground under his hoofs again. I swung into the saddle and continued on my way.

The Wolf And The Sled

Since it is not customary to ride in the saddle in Russia, I bought a small sled, hitched my horse to it, and we trotted merrily on towards St. Petersburg. Somewhere in Esthonia or Latvia, I no longer remember exactly where, but at any rate in a wild, boundless forest, my horse suddenly grew restless. As though lashed by a terrible fear, he broke into a furious gallop. I turned around and saw a gigantic wolf, half mad from hunger, pursuing us, and drawing closer and closer.

Escaping him was hopeless. He was already no more than five yards behind us. So I threw myself full length on the floor of the sled, dropping the reins. And the wolf, who had intended me as his meal, leaped clean over me and swallowed the horse in just a few big swallows. Of course the harness fell onto him, so there he was pulling the sled instead of my horse.

I sat up again, seized the whip, and lashed away at the wolf. He did not like that at all, and my arm still aches when I recall how I pounded away at him with the whip for hours, without a pause.

We flew along through the forest and over the fields, and then we galloped past the first houses of a great city. This was St. Petersburg, and the people on the streets were very surprised. A wolf pulling a sled was something they had never seen before.

The Hard-Drinking General

Immediately after my arrival in St. Petersburg I applied for an officer's commission. But it took quite a time before I received my appointment in the Russian army. Consequently, I had ample time and opportunity to spend my money. We played cards and we drank a great deal, for you know it is very cold during the long Russian winter, and drinking is one way to keep warm. I observed that people who drank too much had an amazing talent for never stopping. I could get drunk just watching them. For instance, there was a general I knew, with a grey beard and a coppery red complexion. In the war with the Turks a sabre stroke had taken the top of his head clean off, so he always wore his hat at table. During a meal he would empty at least three bottles of vodka, and follow that up with a bottle of cognac. Sometimes he would make it two bottles of cognac. But no matter how much he drank, I never saw him drunk.

His capacity remained a mystery to me until one day I learned his strange secret. Every hour or so the general was in the habit of lifting his hat slightly. One evening I noticed that he lifted not only the hat, but a silver plate attached to it, which served him as an artificial scalp. In this curious way the alcohol vapor rose up like a cloud out of his head, and he would be once more as sober as at the beginning of the meal.

My friends would not believe me when I gave them this explanation. So, one day I stepped behind the general just as he lifted his hat, and held a lighted match in the middle of the rising cloud of alcohol vapor. What a sight that was! The cloud caught fire at once and floated, with bluish flames, like a saint's halo above the old gentleman's hat.

Everyone was astonished. The general himself was quite pleased with my little experiment, and I was allowed to repeat it frequently. In fact, he often came to me, pleading: "Münchhausen, light me up again, will you please. I feel like being a floating flame."

The Ducks On The String, And Other Hunting Stories

While hunting one morning I noticed several dozen wild ducks swimming peacefully about on a small lake. If I had shot at any one of them, the others would have flown off, and of course I did not want that to happen. Fortunately, I had an inspiration. I unraveled a long dog-leash made of cord, and knotted the pieces together so

that it was four times as long as it had been. Then to one end I tied a piece of bacon left over from my breakfast. I hid among the reeds, and cautiously trailed the line out into the water. The first duck promptly swam up and swallowed the bacon. Since it was very smooth and slippery, it came out at the other end of the duck,

still attached to the string. The next duck sailed right up and swallowed the piece of bacon, and once more the bait came out behind. So it went, with the bacon passing through all the ducks without the cord breaking. They were lined up on it like pearls on a string.

I drew my string of ducks to land, wound the cord around my body five or six times, and started for home. The ducks were quite heavy, and I was beginning to feel very tired when the ducks, who were all still alive, suddenly began to flap their wings, and rose into the air. They took me right along with them, for I had the line wound around my middle. They wanted to head back toward the lake, but I used my long coat tails as a rudder and forced them to steer inland, until we were fairly close to my home. Then I tied the wings of first one duck, then a second, and so on till I had done them all, and so I dropped gently and slowly down upon my house. I fell right through the chimney, and landed on the kitchen stove — which was where the ducks were meant to end up anyhow. I can tell you, my cook was quite surprised. Fortunately for me, he had not yet lighted the fire in the stove. Otherwise there might have been roast Münchhausen instead roast duck.

Another time, in the same hunting grounds, I unexpectedly came across a splendid stag. As luck would have it, just that very morning I had used up my last bullet. The handsome animal seemed to sense this, for instead of running away he stood staring brashly into my face. Angered by his impudence, I loaded my gun with powder, strewed on top of it a handful of cherry pits I happened to have in my pocket, aimed between the stag's antlers, and fired. He staggered as though momentarily stunned, then bounded away.

A couple of years later I was once again hunting in the same district, and suddenly what should I see before me but a splendid stag with an actual cherry tree growing between his antlers. Well, I thought, this time you

won't escape me. I killed him with a clean shot in the shoulder blade. And since his cherry tree was laden with cherries, the following Sunday I had venison roast with cherry pie. It was a delicious meal, I assure you.

One day a terrible wolf attacked me with such suddenness that I did not have a chance to shoot. In my haste I rammed my fist down his yawning jaws. I kept pushing deeper and deeper; what else could I do? Finally I had my arm right inside the horrible beast, as far as the shoulder. There I was face to face with a wolf whose mouth was foaming and whose flaming eyes blazed with the wish to kill. I can tell you, I did not feel very well. Not a bit. Since I saw no way out of it, I grabbed the wolf's inners, turned him inside out like a glove, tossed him aside, and went on my way, in pretty good spirits.

Once I pursued a hare for two days. My dog kept catching up to it, but I never could get a shot at the animal. It bordered on witchcraft, and although I did not believe in such nonsense, I could think of no other explanation. At last I got a good shot at it, and managed to make a hit. The dog brought him back — and what do you think I saw. In addition to the usual four legs, the hare had two forelegs and two hindlegs on its back. When the two lower pairs were tired, he would flip himself over like a swimmer and run on his back. Well, I had got him anyway, and my dinner guests appreciated the extra four legs. There was a portion more for everybody.

As a matter of fact, my getting a shot at him was not to my credit, but to that of my dog. The dog I owned at the time was a greyhound. He had the greatest speed and endurance I have ever seen in a dog. He ran so often, so fast and so long that in time he wore his legs down to his belly. During the last years of his life I could use him only as a badger-dog — what we call a dachshund. But even as a badger-dog he was first rate. I shall always honor his memory.

The Divided Lithuanian

It is no great loss that none of you knew Count Przo-
bofsky of Lithuania. But his magnificent country estate,
and above all his famous stable, was worth knowing.
His breed of horses, who were known simply as "Lith-
uanians," were worth their weight in gold.

One fine day when I was having tea at the Count's, he
went out into the yard with some gentlemen to show
them one of his young horses. I stayed in the reception
hall with the ladies, entertaining them with some of my
stories. Suddenly we heard panic-stricken cries. I raced
down the stairs into the yard and saw a horse kicking so
wildly that no one dared approach it, let alone mount
it. That was just to my taste. With one leap I was upon
his back, and in a short time had him responding like a
lamb. Training horses is just a matter of knowing how
to ride!

After a few practice leaps, I forced the mount to jump
through the open window into the reception hall, and
then right on to the tea table, where I showed off some
of the tricks of the Spanish Riding School. My horse

went through the whole performance so skillfully that
not a cup was broken. The ladies were delighted, and
the count was so enthusiastic that he asked me to take
the Lithuanian as a gift. I was very glad to have it, since

I was just about to join the Turkish campaign under Field Marshal Münnich.

Two months later, when we drove the Turks into the fortress town of Ochakov, I was in the advance guard and got into trouble because of my Lithuanian's speed. I followed close behind the enemy, and when I saw that he did not intend to hold the fortress but went right on fleeing, I stopped in the marketplace and looked around. I had far outdistanced everyone; neither the trumpeter nor my own Hussars were in sight. Accordingly, I rode my Lithunian to the fountain in the marketplace and let him drink. He drank and drank, but seemed unable to quench his thirst. Finally I reached back to give him a reassuring pat on the crupper — and struck empty air. I turned around in surprise — and my mouth flew open. What do you think I saw? Nothing at all. The hindpart of the poor beast, his haunches and hind legs, were quite gone, as if cut clean off. The water which he had been drinking was simply flowing out again behind.

While I was trying to think how this could have happened, my groom came galloping up to me and breathlessly explained. As I rode through the fortress behind

the fleeing enemy, the gates had been dropped and had cut the hind part of the horse clean off. This part had trotted off to a nearby meadow where some other horses were grazing. We would probably find it there, my groom said.

We galloped like the wind back to the meadow and there, sure enough, we found the hind half of the Lithuanian cavorting about in the grass as spry as you please. I was overjoyed. I sent for the regimental blacksmith at once. Without more ado, he stitched the two parts together with some young laurel shoots which happened to be at hand. The wound healed in a few days. And by and by something happened which was well merited by so glorious a horse. The shoots started to grow and form a kind of laurel wreath over the animal's back, and thereafter I rode about the country with this evergreen canopy protecting me from the heat of the sun.

The Ride On Cannonball, And
Other Adventures

During the same campaign we beseiged a city — I have been at so many sieges I've forgotten now which city it was — but it was very well defended. Marshal Münnich was eager to know what was going on inside the fort. But it was impossible for us to get through the advance guards, the ditches and the cavalry obstacles.

I was young then, and brimming with eagerness to do my duty. So without thinking the matter through, I stood by one of our biggest cannon, which was bombarding the city. When it was fired, I leaped on the cannonball as it came hissing out of the barrel. My intention was to ride the ball right into the fortress. But during the roaring flight through the air my doubts began to mount. Getting in is going to be easy, I thought, but how am I going to get out again. As soon as they catch sight of my uniform they will recognize me for an enemy and hang me from the nearest tree.

These thoughts worried me exceedingly. And when a Turkish cannonball aimed at our camp flew by me, I

swung over on to it and returned to my Hussars, without having accomplished my purpose, but at least safe and in high spirits.

There was no animal like my horse for jumping over fences, walls and ditches. Obstacles simply did not exist for us. Once, when I was following a hare, my quarry ran across a highway. Just at that moment a coach containing two lovely ladies crossed my path. Since the coach windows were down, and I did not want to abandon my pursuit of the hare, I sent my horse jumping right through the coach. We passed through so fast that

I barely had time to lift my hat and apologize to the ladies for disturbing them.

Another time I wanted to jump my Lithuanian across a marsh. Midway in the leap I realized that the marsh was a good deal wider than I had anticipated. I turned my steed around in midair, and we landed safely on dry

land. On the second try we again jumped short, and sank up to our necks in the mud, not far from the opposite shore. We would have died miserably had I not acted quick as thought; my hand flew to my head, and I pulled myself up out of the marsh by my own pigtail. And not only myself, but my horse as well. Muscular strength is a great help in time of need.

In spite of my own bravery and intelligence, and my Lithuanian's speed and endurance, I one day found myself in battle with immensely superior forces, and was taken prisoner. Worse still, I was sold as a slave. That was a real misfortune, although my work could not really be called hard labor. It was not strange, but rather ridiculous. Every morning I had to drive the Turkish sultan's bees out to pasture. There I had to guard them through the day as if they were sheep or goats, and in the evening I was required to shoo them back to their hives.

One evening I saw that two bears had attacked one of my bees, and were on the point of tearing it to pieces for the honey it had collected. I had nothing in my hands but the silver ax which the sultan's gardeners carried as

a sign of their office. Accordingly, I threw the ax with all my might at the two bears. It missed them, but I had flung it with such tremendous force that it continued to fly on, higher and higher. Can you guess where it landed? On the moon!

What was I to do? How could I get it back again? Where would I find ladders long enough? Luckily, I remembered that Turkish beans grow to amazing heights in a very short time, because of the hot climate. I promptly planted a bean. Sure enough, it grew right up to the moon and wound around one tip of the moon's crescent. Nothing was easier than to climb the beanstalk hand over hand, and half an hour later I found my ax lying on a heap of chaff and straw. I was much relieved, and thought I would climb back down to Turkey at once. But alas, the sun's heat had completely dried out my beanstalk, and I felt sure it would not support me. Without more ado, I wove a rope out of the moonstraw, and tied it to one of the horns of the moon. Then I cautiously let myself down. After a while, I cut off the extra portion of rope above my head, which I no longer needed, and knotted it to the bottom of my rope. All went well for quite a while, but suddenly, while I was still hanging in the clouds, the rope broke. I fell down to God's green earth with such force that I plunged thirty feet deep into the ground. Every bone in my body ached. But after I had recovered somewhat, I used my fingernails — which luckily I had not cut for ten years – to carve out a kind of staircase in the ground, climbed up these stairs, and so returned to my bees.

The next time I went out, I found a cleverer way to deal with the bears. I rubbed the shaft of a farm wagon with honey, and concealed myself in the bushes nearby. Soon a gigantic bear appeared, lured by the smell of the honey, and began licking away at the shaft so greedily that he gradually rammed the shaft through his throat, stomach and intestines and out behind again. There he was, spitted on the shaft. I rushed up, hammered a peg through the end of the shaft, and left Master Bear kicking there until the next morning. The sultan, who chanced to walk by, almost split his sides laughing.

Shortly afterwards, the Russians and the Turks made peace, and I was one of the first prisoners to be released and sent back to St. Petersburg. There I resigned my commission and returned to Germany. The winter was so severe that even the sun developed chilblains, and I suffered horribly from the cold.

Since my Lithuanian had been kept by the Turks, I had to travel by the mail sled. Riding down a road with

steep snowbanks towering on either side, I asked the postillion to blow his horn, to warn any vehicles from the opposite direction that we were coming. He put the horn to his lips and blew with all his might. But no matter how hard he tried, not a sound came out. We reached the next station safe and sound, and decided to rest and warm up there. The postillion hung his horn on a nail near the kitchen stove, and we sat down to eat.

Suddenly we heard, "Tayreng, tayreng, tayreng, tengteng!" We opened our ears and eyes. Then we realized why the postillion had been unable to blow the horn earlier. The notes had frozen fast inside the horn. Now they were thawing out one after the other, and providing us with a regular dinner concert. We heard "John Peel" and "Greensleeves" and the beautiful old song, "The Earl of Moray."

That is the end of the story of my Russian travels. If you think I have been exaggerating a little here and there, I advise you to listen no more. Because the adventures I had afterwards were even more remarkable, and not a bit less true.

The Wager With The Sultan

Years later I went to Turkey again. This time I was not a prisoner of war, but a man of rank and title. Several ambassadors introduced me to the sultan, who asked me to undertake an important secret mission to Cairo for him. I consented, and shortly afterwards set off in great pomp, with a large retinue.

As soon as we left Constantinople, I saw a small, thin man running rapidly as a weasel across a field. When we approached closer, I saw to my astonishment that he had lead weights attached to each leg. They must have been at least fifty pounds each. "What's the hurry?" I called out. "And why the weights?"

"Oh," he said, "I ran away from Vienna half an hour ago and am going to Constantinople to look for a new job. I'm wearing the weights in order not to run too fast. I'm in no hurry."

Here was a useful fellow, I thought. I asked whether he would care to travel with me. We soon came to an agreement on his wages, and he came along with us.

We passed through many a country and many a city. One day I saw a man lying in a meadow near the side of the road. He had his ear pressed to the ground as though he were eavesdropping on a conversation among the moles.

"What are you doing?" I asked.

"Listening to the grass grow," he replied.

"Can you really hear that?" I asked.

"Nothing to it for me," he replied, shrugging. I hired him on the spot. People who can hear the grass grow are always useful.

That was a lucky day for me altogether. On a hill I noticed a hunter with a rifle who seemed to be shooting holes in the air. "What's the idea?" I asked. "What are you shooting at?"

"Oh," he said, "I'm just trying out my new rifle
was a sparrow sitting on top of the tower of Str
cathedral, and I just shot it down."

Naturally, I took this hunter with me.

We rode on and on, and one day we came
Mountain of Lebanon. There, just on the outsk
cedar grove, stood a stocky, powerful-looking
pulling on a rope which he had slung around th
grove. "What is the idea?" I asked in amazeme

"Oh," he replied, "I was sent out for wood

got to bring my axe." As he spoke, he pulled down the entire grove, which was at least two acres. Naturally, I took him along too. He demanded the high wages which men in heavy industry get, but I would not have left him in Lebanon if it had cost me my entire salary as an ambassador.

When we reached Egypt, we were suddenly caught in so terrible a storm that our horses and wagons were knocked over, and we were almost lifted into the air. Nearby stood six windmills whirling like mad. And at some distance from them stood a thick-set fellow hold-

ing his right nostril shut with his finger. When he saw us being flipped and flopped about by the wind, he took his finger from his nose and politely doffed his hat. Suddenly not a breath of air was stirring, and all six windmills stood still.

"Are you the Devil's uncle?" I called out in some anger.

"I beg your pardon, your Excellency," he replied. "I was only making a little wind for the miller. If I don't hold my right nostril shut, the windmills would be blown off the map."

I took him into my employ on the spot.

We continued on to Cairo. When I had completed my secret mission, I discharged my entire retinue, keeping in my service only the swift runner, the listener, the hunter, the strong man of Lebanon, and the wind-maker.

After my mission to Egypt I rose even higher than before in the sultan's favor. Each day we had our noon and evening meals together, and I must say, his cuisine was better than that of all the other monarchs I have ever dined with. But the drinks were another matter — oh dear! For as everyone knows, Moslems are not allowed to drink wine. I minded this a good deal. And it appeared to me that the sultan did, too.

One day after luncheon he secretly signed to me to follow him into a small private room. After he had bolted the door, he took a bottle out of a cupboard, saying, "This is my last bottle of Hungarian Tokay wine. Christians certainly know a thing or two about drinking, and I've heard that you are an expert, Münchhausen. But I'll wager you have never drunk anything so delicious in your life."

He poured us each a glass, and we drank. "Well, what do you think of it?" he asked triumphantly.

"A decent lesser wine," I replied. "Still, I've drunk some a good deal better at the table of Emperor Charles the Sixth in Vienna. Your Majesty should taste one of his some day."

"I respect your opinions, Baron. But there is no better Tokay. It was given to me by a Hungarian count who told me that it was the best in the world."

"What will you wager?" I cried. "In an hour I will fetch a bottle from the imperial cellars in Vienna that will make you open your eyes."

"Münchhausen, you're talking nonsense."

"I am not talking nonsense, your Majesty. In sixty minutes a bottle from the imperial cellars in Vienna will stand here on this table, and compared to it you will think this wine is plain vinegar."

The sultan waved his finger threateningly at me. "You are trying to play a joke on me, Münchhausen. I will not stand for that. I know that you are generally an exceptionally truthful man, but this time you are fabricating, Baron."

"Try me," I said. "If I do not keep my word, your Majesty may have my head cut off. And let me tell you, I prize my head. What will you bet against it?"

"I'll take you at your word," the sultan replied. "I don't like my friends to make game of me. If that bottle is not on the table at the stroke of four, you lose your head. But if you win the wager, you may take as much gold, silver, pearls and diamonds from my treasure chamber as the strongest man can manage to carry."

"Done!" I exclaimed. "A fair bet." Thereupon I asked for pen and ink and wrote the following letter to Empress Maria Theresa: "As the heiress of your noble late father, your Majesty has undoubtedly inherited his wine cellar. May I ask you to give my messenger a bottle of your Tokay from it? But please, give him only the very best, for I have staked my head on the quality of your wine. My warmest thanks in advance. Yours sincerely, Baron Münchhausen."

I gave this missive to my fast runner. He unbuckled his lead weights, and instantly set out. It was then five minutes past three. The sultan and I sat drinking the rest of the bottle, and glancing up occasionally at the clock. Three-fifteen. Three-thirty. When the clock struck three-forty-five and there was no sign of my runner, I began to feel a mite worried. The sultan was already eyeing the bell cord. Soon he would ring for his executioner.

I asked for permission to go for a walk in the garden. The sultan nodded, but he ordered several guards to stay at my heels. At three-fifty I became so nervous that I sent for my listener and my hunter. The listener threw himself flat on the ground, and presently announced that the runner was far away, lying sound asleep and snoring mightily. The sharpshooter ran up on a high terrace, peered through the sight of his rifle, and called down in high indignation. "Sure enough, there he lies. Under an oak tree near Belgrade. And the bottle of Tokay is right beside him. You wait, my fine fellow." Then he took aim and fired into the air.

What do you think happened? The bullet struck the oak under which the runner lay snoring. Twigs and acorns showered down upon his face. He jumped to his feet, picked up the bottle, and arrived at five minutes before four in front of the sultan's private room. What a weight that was off my heart.

The sultan was all eagerness to sample the Tokay. "I have lost the wager, Münchhausen," he then announced. After locking the bottle carefully away in his cupboard, he rang for the treasurer and said: "My friend Münchhausen has permission to take as many valuables from the treasury as the strongest man can carry away." The treasurer bowed until his nose touched the ground. The sultan shook hands heartily with me, and dismissed us both.

Now there was no time to be lost. I called my strong man and hustled to the treasury with him. With long ropes, he tied up an enormous bundle. The amount of pearls, diamonds, silver and gold he did not manage to include in that bundle was scarcely worth mentioning. Then we immediately raced down to the harbor, rented the biggest sailing vessel we could find, lifted anchor, and made for the open sea. And none too soon. For when the sultan heard about the trick I had played on him, he ordered the grand admiral to sail out with the entire Turkish navy, and capture my ship.

We were barely two miles away from the coast when I saw the Turkish navy approaching under full sail. I must admit that my head began to feel unsteady on my shoulders once again. But my wind-maker said, "Don't worry, your Excellency." He stepped out on the after-deck and held his head in such a position that his right nostril was directed toward the Turkish fleet and his left nostril toward our sails. And then he blew such violent blasts that the fleet was driven back into port with splintered masts and tattered sails, while our vessel shot over the waves as if it had wings, and we arrived in Italy only three hours later.

The Second Voyage To The Moon

Do you remember how I had to climb up to the moon in order to retrieve my silver axe? Well, later on I paid another visit to the moon, although in far more pleasant a fashion. A distant kinsman of mine, a very rich man, was planning an expedition. There must be a country inhabited by giants, he said, like the Kingdom of Brobdingnag which Gulliver has told about. This country he was determined to find and asked me to accompany him. I thought the whole business a fable, but I knew he had made me his heir, and so I felt I owed him a small favor or two.

So we set out and reached the South Seas without seeing anything worth mentioning, except for a few flying men and women who danced minuets in the air. Our real adventures did not begin until the eighteenth day after we passed the island of Otaheiti. Then we ran into an uncanny hurricane which lifted our ship about a thousand miles into the air. High above the clouds, we sailed for six weeks and a day, favored by a steady wind, until we came upon a vast land. It was round and glistening, and resembled a shining island. We anchored in a comfortable harbor and went on land. Far below us we saw through our telescopes the globe of the earth, with its lakes, rivers, mountains and cities, all small as toys.

The island, we soon realized, was the moon. The natives rode through the air on three-headed vultures, just as if these were horses. Since there happened to be a war on against the sun, the king of the moon offered me a commission in his army. I declined, however, when I heard that large white radishes were used in place of spears, and mushrooms as shields. A vegetarian war was not my dish of tea, I said.

In addition to the giants of the moon, I also met the inhabitants of the Dog Star. They are busy traveling salesmen, and journey around the whole universe. They look something like large bulldogs, and have their eyes below their noses. Since they have no eyelids, these people cover their eyes with their tongues when they go to sleep. The natives of the Dog Star are on the average

twenty feet high, the moon people thirty-six feet. Their name for themselves, however, is not moon men, but "cooking creatures," because they prepare their food on stoves, just as we do. They eat differently, however, and much faster than we. They simply open up their left side and shove their meals directly into their stomachs. This, they do only once a month, or twelve times a year.

In other respects, too, they have an easy life. Animals on the moon and even the "cooking creatures" themselves, grow on trees, inside six-foot-long, nutlike fruits which are plucked when ripe, stored for a time, and finally dropped into hot water. After a few hours, the ripe creatures jump out. Each of these creatures is prepared before birth for his future profession, whether it is soldier, teacher, preacher or farmer, and he begins to ply his trade immediately upon birth.

The moon men have only one finger on each hand. They carry their heads under their arms, and when they go traveling or to work, normally leave their heads home. They can reverse this process, however, and send the head out, leaving the body at home. They can take their eyes in their hands and see just as well with them as if the eyes were still in their heads. When they lose an eye, it does not matter. New eyes can be bought in specialty shops. They come in all colors, and are not too expensive. When I was on the moon, yellow eyes were very much in fashion.

Before I forget: their stomachs serve the moon people as knapsacks and handbags. They tuck everything they need to carry into their stomachs, which can be opened and closed at will. When they grow old, they do not die, but dissolve into the air and fly off above the rooftops like smoke.

I must admit that all this sounds very queer. But it is true all the same, and anyone who doubts one single detail need only go to the moon and check up on everything I have said. Then he will have to apologize to me, and pronounce that my account is not a whit less truthful than the stories of all other moon-voyages. All my life I have hated big, whopping lies. I can't help it; that's just the way I am. And now, since I'm thirsty from so much story telling, I'm going to drink a glass of punch.

Waiter, fill my three-gallon glass. Cheers!